BEN & EMMA'S BIG HIT

Written by GAVIN NEWSOM with RUBY SHAMIR

Illustrated by ALEXANDRA THOMPSON

PHILOMEL

When Ben walked up to home plate to bat, he saw everything.

He saw the diamond-shaped field.

He saw the dome of the pitcher's mound.

He saw the curve of the ball as it left the player's hands.

All those shapes told a story to Ben—a story about playing the very best game of baseball he could.

But there were other shapes that didn't make as much sense to Ben.

When he looked at a book, he knew there was a story in it too, but he had a hard time figuring it out because he had dyslexia.

That's why Ms. Kim coached him in reading. Just like Ben's Little League coach trained his team in baseball, Ms. Kim trained her team of students in reading by connecting letters to their sounds.

She taught him the letter "B" made a sound like a sheep, BAA! It was confusing because when he learned his ABC's, he made a BEE sound! Ben didn't like this one bit.

Ss Tt Uu Vv Ww Xx Yy Zz

Today is: Wednesday
Words of the day

Ball
Bat
Hit

MS. KIM

Reading time was Ben's least favorite part of the day. It seemed so easy for everyone else, like Emma, the star pitcher of his baseball team, who was in his reading group. She always walked around with the biggest, fattest chapter books. Ben had trouble with even the shortest words.

On the ball field, everything seemed to click into place for Ben and he felt cool and calm. But when it was time for reading groups, he felt very different. His belly ached and he started to sweat. It felt like going up against the hardest team in the league, every day.

The reading group started with an alphabet drill. When they got to the letter "B," Ms. Kim held up a picture of a bat. Ben smiled for a moment.

"What are you thinking about, Ben?" Ms. Kim asked.

"A home run," Ben said.
"The bat reminded me."

"I think the letter 'B' looks like a bat with two baseballs," Emma added.

They finished the alphabet and then Ms. Kim started putting letters together into words for Ben and Emma to practice reading.

BAT

BALL

HIT

But Ben didn't read words like he knew he was supposed to. He wasn't able to connect the letters to their sounds. Nothing made any sense.

"B-a-t, bat," Emma said when she looked at the first word Ms. Kim had put up.

"Good," Ms. Kim said. Emma smiled.

"How did you know that?" Ben whispered to Emma.

"I remembered it from this morning," she whispered back.

Ben slumped in his chair. He felt all alone.

Ms. Kim put up different letter cards. "Ben, how about this one?"

Ben stared hard at the letter cards. His face got hot. His mouth felt dry. He hoped that the word would just pop into his head. But it didn't.

The lines said nothing. The circles said nothing. Just like yesterday and the day before and the day before that.

He couldn't stay in the room, not one second more.

So he ran. Like he was rounding the bases, trying to beat the ball home, he ran right out the door.

Ms. Kim found Ben by the water fountain.

"I was thirsty," Ben mumbled, but he wasn't. He was upset. He was embarrassed. And he didn't like reading.

"Would you like to take a couple of deep breaths?" Ms. Kim asked.

He did.

Soon, Ben and Ms. Kim walked back into the classroom.

"Learning to read can be tough,"
Ms. Kim said.

"Not for Emma," Ben said. "She always
takes out the biggest books from the
library."

"I do like big books," Emma said
quietly. "But I can't read them. Not
yet, anyway."

"So why do you always pick
them?" Ben asked.

"I like to pretend I can," Emma
said. Tears pooled in her eyes. She
blinked them back, but Ben had
already noticed.

"I'm sorry," Ben said. He had never seen Emma get upset.

"It's okay," Emma said, wiping away a tear.

"I didn't know," Ben said. "You are always great at everything you do."

"So are you, Ben," Emma said. "You hit home runs almost every game."

"I guess," Ben said. "But baseball is fun."

"Even so," Ms. Kim said, "you have to practice and try hard, right?"

Ben nodded.

"When we practice reading, you show yourself every day how hard you can try," Ms. Kim said.

Ms. Kim taught Ben and Emma to sound out letters to read the word "hit."

"When I was a kid, I never once got a hit," Ms. Kim said.

"Really?" Ben and Emma couldn't believe it.

"Never," Ms. Kim said. "I loved baseball, but reading came easier to me than hitting ever did."

Ben and Emma looked at each other. Then Ben said, "Maybe we can teach you—at recess?"

Ms. Kim thought about it for a moment. "I'd really like that," she said.

Emma told the rest of the class about the plan for recess. They all came to cheer on their teacher.

Ms. Kim was nervous.

"You can do this," Ben told her.

He stood behind her to play catcher. Emma pitched. Ms. Kim missed. Strike one.

"My coach always tells me to take deep breaths and watch the ball," Ben said to Ms. Kim.

"Okay, got it. I'm ready for another
one," Ms. Kim called to Emma.

Emma threw another pitch to Ms. Kim.

Again Ms. Kim missed. Strike two.

"This is really hard," Ms. Kim said.

"You told me, show yourself how hard you can try,"
Ben said.

Ms. Kim smiled. "You're right," she said.

Ben showed Ms. Kim every step he took when he
hit a home run. Ms. Kim practiced a few times.

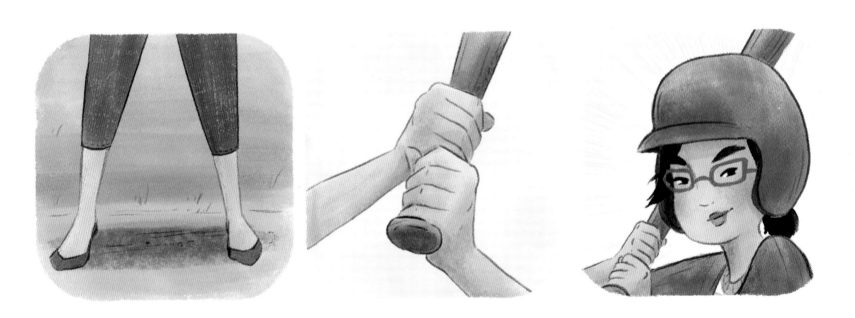

"Ready?" Emma asked.

"Sure am!" Ms. Kim called back.

Clutching her bat, Ms. Kim watched as the ball flew toward her.

She swung and—CRACK—the bat made contact with the ball. It didn't go very far, but Ms. Kim had hit the ball!

"You did it!" Ben and Emma yelled.

"I did! I can't believe it!" Ms. Kim said.

"What a relief. My stomach was in knots!"

"I know all about that feeling," Ben said.

Ben and Emma's classmates flooded the field, high-fiving and cheering.

As Ben took in the scene, he saw all the same familiar shapes he knew so well.

But he also saw another story unfold—the story of someone who tried really hard and found her own way to learn something new.

"You never gave up, Ms. Kim," Ben said.

"You didn't let me, Coach!"

And Ben knew that he'd never let himself give up either. He would get help from his team. Even if learning to read was hard, he'd keep on trying. Every day.

Dear Reader,

When I was ten years old, I was snooping around my mom's bedroom when I noticed some papers that had my name on them. As I flipped through the pages, I saw one word pop up over and over again: "dyslexia."

When I asked my mom about it, she explained that I had been diagnosed with dyslexia, but she hadn't wanted to tell me. Back when I was a kid, having dyslexia was something to hide; it was considered shameful. But uncovering the truth about my trouble with reading was actually a relief. I finally understood why I couldn't coast through my homework like my sister. I finally understood that I was smart, just as smart as any of my speed-reading classmates, but that my brain worked differently from people without dyslexia.

In order to crack the code of the written word, I would have to work a hundred times harder, and use a million strategies and techniques that people with non-dyslexic brains don't even have to consider. I had to learn to read "the way an athlete pushes himself beyond where it is comfortable to go," as the poet Philip Schultz wrote about his dyslexia.

Over time, I realized that challenging my brain this intensely actually helped me in ways I never expected. My brain had to leap, jump, and zigzag to decode every word, which sparked my creativity. I had to learn by heart just about everything I read, which sharpened my memory. I had to overcome the dread of potential embarrassment, which made me more bold, more fearless. In short, I realized that my dyslexia was a gift.

And yours can be too. Yes, you will make mistakes—who doesn't? And reading will probably always be tough—it still is for me. But those challenges are also your strengths. You think differently, and the world needs your creative problem-solving. You know frustration, and the world needs your caring, kindness, and patience for others who are struggling. You know how to try really hard, and the world needs your effort and skills to make it a better place. YOU are the very type of leader our world needs, and I can't wait to see where your talents will take you!

Yours,

For every kid who struggles with dyslexia or
any learning disability, you can be anything
you want to be; don't let anyone tell you
that you have limits in life.

For my children, Montana, Hunter, Brooklynn,
and Dutch, who have taught me more about
life and what's important than anyone else.

And for my incredible wife, Jen, whose grace
and passion have made my life whole.
—G. N.

For Mrs. Chase.
—A. T.

RESOURCES

International Dyslexia Association: www.dyslexiaida.org

National Center on Improving Literacy: www.improvingliteracy.org

Understood: www.understood.org

The Yale Center for Dyslexia & Creativity: www.dyslexia.yale.edu

BOOK: *Overcoming Dyslexia: Second Edition*

ACKNOWLEDGMENTS

I dealt with a learning curve when putting this book together and have a newfound respect for
children's book authors who often don't get the credit they deserve for their work.

Thank you to my friend Yashar Ali, who inspired this book and pushed me to publish it.

Thank you to my co-author Ruby Shamir, who brought this story to life in a way I couldn't have
imagined.

Thank you to the illustrator of this book, the incredibly talented Alexandra Thompson, whose
illustrations have brought such wonderful depth to this story, especially since those of us who are
dyslexic rely so much on visual aids.

I'm grateful to the team at Penguin, especially Jill Santopolo, for their dedication and tenacity
and for putting up with a first-time children's book author.

Thank you to Sally Shaywitz, MD, and the other dyslexia experts I consulted for their help in
making this book as accurate as possible.

This is my third project with my longtime literary agent Elyse Cheney, who is, as always, loyal,
brilliant, and unflappable. Thank you, Elyse.

PHILOMEL BOOKS
An imprint of Penguin Random House LLC, New York

First published in the United States of America by Philomel,
an imprint of Penguin Random House LLC, 2021.

Text copyright © 2021 by Gavin Newsom. • Illustrations copyright © 2021 by Alexandra Thompson.

Philomel Books is a registered trademark of Penguin Random House LLC.

Visit us online at penguinrandomhouse.com.

Library of Congress Cataloging-in-Publication Data is available.

Manufactured in China.

ISBN 9780593204115

1 3 5 7 9 10 8 6 4 2

Edited by Jill Santopolo. • Design by Ellice M. Lee. • Text set in Open Dyslexie.